For Adam and Thomas
who inspired it,
and Finn
who arrived just in time

First published in Great Britain in 1988 by
The Bodley Head Ltd.

Library of Congress Catalog Card Number 88-81802

ISBN 0-316-14498-3

10 9 8 7 6 5 4 3 2 1

Printed and bound in Italy

THE STORY OF HORRIBLE HILDA AND HENRY

EMMA CHICHESTER CLARK

Little, Brown and Company

Boston   Toronto   London

Hilda and Henry Hatter were two thoroughly horrible children. They made their parents' lives miserable.

It was after they had painted the new wallpaper green . . .

and each other purple, that Mr. and Mrs. Hatter decided to give them to a zoo.

The zookeeper was delighted. It was a long time since he had had any new animals.

The giraffes and elephants were not so pleased to see them.

Hilda and Henry threw their food around and danced on their backs.

They were mean to the snakes . . .

teased the poor penguins . . .

and pestered the kiwis and ostriches with their silly games.

They almost deafened the parrots
and they dive-bombed the seals.

In the monkey enclosure, Hilda and Henry were abominable.
They gobbled up all their bananas and shocked the visitors
as they swung about and screamed and shouted. They were
wilder than any of the animals in the zoo.

Eventually the animals complained to the zookeeper.
He was very, very angry.

"That is ENOUGH!" he shouted. "The fun and games are over!"

grrrrrrr

He put the children into a cage with a bad-tempered lion named
Brian. For once in their lives, Hilda and Henry were frightened,
and for the first time since they had arrived at the zoo,

they wished they could go home. Brian had a ferocious appetite.
After he had finished his dinner, he ate . . .

Hilda's and Henry's as well. The children were too frightened to complain.

They grew thinner and thinner, and more and more worried.

Brian's roar made their hair stand on end.

They wished now that they hadn't been so horrible. In all their lives they had never ever done a single thing that they were told, and now they were sorry.

One day Mr. and Mrs. Hatter came to visit Hilda and Henry and were amazed by the changes they saw. They decided to take the children home.

They invited Brian to come and look after Hilda and Henry,

just in case they began to slip back into their old ways.

Hilda and Henry became considerate and helpful,
obedient and kind.

Brian was fond of them now that they were nicer.
They even brushed their teeth and went to bed on time.

"In fact," as Brian said to Mrs. Hatter one day, "no one would ever guess just how horrible Hilda and Henry used to be."